ATLANTIS RISING

BOOK ONE
THE MISSION

BILL CRAIG

DEDICATION:

For the Ahern Family, Sharon,
Samantha, Jason, this one is for you
in memory of Jerry. With Love.

Also for my Children and
Grandchildren, You Are The Future!

Top secret:

   Atlantis Geo-thermal science center has recently discovered that the geo-thermal vents that have provided energy to the five undersea cities making up the nation of Atlantis are crumbling and within the year will fail, leaving the dome cities without out power or heat. Surface colonization is now, after 500 years, our only hope of survival.

Dr. Arthur Roddenberry
Geo-thermal Science Unit,
Atlantica Dome.

"Mister President, Dr. Roddenberry is here to see you,' Chief of Staff Arnold Putnam announced, opening the oak door to the Oval Office.

"Show him in Arnold, then leave us alone," President Michael Shaw replied, not turning around. President Shaw continued to look out on the ocean beyond the transparent aluminum dome.

"Yes Sir," Putnam replied. He heard soft voices and then the door closed. President Shaw turned, facing his visitor for the first time. Dr. Roddenberry was a thin man with long angular limbs and a thin angular face, high cheekbones, thin lips, brown thinning hair combed over to the left. Intelligent blue eyes behind thick lensed glasses. Roddenberry looked tired, dark circles under his eyes and lines cut deeply into his high forehead.

"Dr. Roddenberry, I presume?" Shaw asked.

"I am," Roddenberry confirmed, taking in the man that was the serving elected President of the undersea nation of Atlantis. In his mid-forties, the President was in surprisingly good shape with thick brown-hair going gray at the temples, brown eyes, and a muscular frame. A mustache covered his upper lip.

"I understand you have some rather grim news for me," President Shaw said, getting right to the point.

"Yes, I'm afraid I do Mr. President. The geo-thermal vents that Atlantis draws its power from are starting to crumble. They are in eminent danger of collapse. When that happens, Atlantis will go dark. No power, no heat," Roddenberry explained.

"How long have you known about this?" Shaw looked at him.

"Three days."

"What took you so long to notify me?"

"This was the earliest I could get an appointment."

"How long do we have before the vent collapses?" Shaw asked, looking annoyed. He an Arnold Putnam were going to have a long talk that Arnold was probably not going to like.

"At most eighteen months, at least six months. Best guess, a year," Roddenberry replied.

"What do you recommend, Doctor?" Shaw asked.

"We have only one choice. The surface."

"We have no idea what we might find out there."

"If we don't go, we die Mr. President. Can you live with that?"

"Put together a team of scientists for the expedition, Doctor. But I want them to know they are to follow orders of the Marines that will be accompanying them. It's time we find out what the U.S.S. Leviathan can really do and see if the expense is justified," President Shaw replied.

"What kind of team, Mr. President?" Roddenberry asked, looking mystified.

"A team that can tell us if the surface is truly habitable again. After 500 years, Doctor, who knows what we might find up there..." Shaw's voice trailed off.

"I'll send a recommendation before the day is out, Mr. President. I just need time to determine what sort of people we need."

"Hand carry the list Dr. Roddenberry. I'll make sure you are ushered in to see me immediately. As you have determined, time is absolutely of the essence."

"Yes Sir, Mr. President," Roddenberry replied and he turned and went out the door, mopping his brow with a handkerchief, his mind racing.

President Shaw walked over to the bar and poured himself a shot of Scotch. He picked up a book he had taken out of the Presidential library after he had seen the first message from Dr. Roddenberry. It was the chronicle of Adam Meacham, the last President of the United States and the first President of Atlantis.

"It was a nightmare time. Between the volcanic eruptions across the country, the category five storms, the earthquakes and tsunamis that were battering the United States. People were dying by the hundreds of thousands. I knew about the Atlantis Project, but I was sworn to secrecy. I let my handlers bundle me onto Airforce One and we lifted off. I watched from the air as

earthquakes shattered Florida and dropped it under the ocean. I saw the tsunamis wipe out life on Bermuda and in the Bahamas, then crash back against the radically changed U.S. Coastline. People were dying and I was powerless to help them.

"Airforce One flew north to Greenland. There was an airstrip cleared there that we could land on. It was in Greenland that I boarded the U.S.S. Endeavour. As we submerged I saw a towering wall of water surging towards us as the submarine slipped beneath the waves. I prayed for those who remained behind because I knew that they were about to die

"It took us nearly a week to reach Atlantis Base. As the submarine docked and I exited the u-boat to enter the base I was amazed.

Never had I seen such wonders. The people who populated the undersea cities were a mixture of scientists, sailors, and common people who could contribute to society. Only two of the domes were full at the moment. But there were seven in all, and I knew that someday they would all be full of life, full of families. Not in my time, perhaps, but someday.

"Today was indeed the first day of the rest of my life. I was the leader of what was left of mankind, and I had a job to do. It was up to me to do it. I prayed that God would lead me as I began to lead this new world beneath the waves."

President Shaw placed his bookmark. He would read more later, but for now, he found himself at a crossroads, the same sort of crossroads that Meacham had found

himself at 500 years ago. Shaw took
another book from his desk. A
family Bible that had been handed
down for more than 700 years.
Shaw laid his hands on the book as
he knelt down in the Oval Office
and he began to pray.

Thomas Seaver stood alone on the shooting range. A pistol lay on the bench before him. It was a copy of a Browning Hi-Power 9mm that had belonged to one of his ancestors. Unlike the more modern pistols, it still fired a bullet out of a brass cartridge filled with gun powder. A man-shaped target hung twenty yards downrange. Seaver pulled the earmuffs over his ears and picked up the gun, working the slide to chamber the top round off the magazine.

Holding the pistol in a modified Weaver stance he raised it until the white dot on the front sight covered the center of mass on the target and his finger slowly squeezed the trigger. The pistol jumped in his fist and a hole appeared in the target. Seaver fired again and again. Soon the center of the target was an open hole.

Thomas Seaver loaded the empty magazine and replaced the pistol into his shooting bag. His wife was less than happy with his current enthusiasm but she would deal with it. Seaver was both biologist and historian. He liked to plan ahead. Atlantis was at best, a short term solution for an ages old problem. Man would eventually have to return to the surface of the earth and Thomas Seaver planned to be ready when they did.

His wife was less a fan of the idea, Thomas knew. Maria believed that man would always remain beneath the waves. She was a botanist, and by virtue of that fact naïve. Maria had no idea what it would mean to go back to he surface. But he did. On the surface there would be a mutated world. Animals, plants, possibly even humans. Some would have survived. What sort of society they would have formed he could only guess at.

Seaver was not naïve enough to believe that the Atlantis Domes were the only place that were prepared for the devastating circumstances that had driven man beneath the waves. No he was sure that other governments, and even groups of like minded people had banded together to survive what they had known was coming.

Seaver had read everything available in Atlantis' vast library about the times and the way nature seemed to be in revolt. Mankind, in its arrogance had tried to rule the earth, and the Earth, a living organism had revolted, scrubbing the over-populated surface free of the infestation of man. He knew that if they were too ever return to the surface, man would have to live in harmony with nature rather than trying to tame it.

"Incoming message," his personal communication device chimed. Seaver reached over to his wrist and tapped the screen, which immediately changed from chronograph to communications mode. "Dr. Seaver, please report at once to Dr. Roddenberry in Geo-science," announced a computer generated voice. Seaver regarded it for a moment.

"I'm on the way," Seaver replied, then tapped the screen to end the transmission. He tapped the screen again. "Maria Seaver, got a summons over to Geo-science, so I'm gonna be late for dinner. Sorry," he said before closing the transmission. Geo-science? What the hell could Roddenberry want with him? Seaver headed for the monorail system that served as public transportation in the United States of Atlantis.

Maria Seaver placed dinner on the table. Another late night for Tom and another meal alone for her. She had hoped to have this night, their wedding anniversary alone with her husband, not eating alone by candlelight. She picked up her goblet of wine and sipped from it.

She had hoped tonight would be different. So much had become strained between them of late, Tom with his predictions of doom and gloom. She shook her head. "Incoming message," her personal communicator chimed for the second time in fifteen minutes. Her forehead wrinkled as she wondered who was calling. She tapped the screen. "Dr. Maria Seaver, please report to Geo-science as soon as possible," the computer generated voice commanded.

"Right away," Maria replied, wondering what the summons was about. Tom had mentioned geo-science in his message. It made her wonder. Maria grabbed a jacket and slipped it on before leaving their apartment, locking the door behind her.

"What is the progress on Leviathan, Admiral?" President Shaw asked.

"She's ready for sea-testing, right on schedule, Mr. President," Admiral James Thatcher replied. Thatcher had been one of the designers of the super-sub that was designed to also serve as a surface-based aircraft carrier.

"Glad to hear it, Jim. However her first sea-trial could be a trial by fire. Pour yourself a drink and have a seat," Michael Shaw pointed at the chair across from his own. He already had a double Scotch on ice in his hand.

Thatcher poured his own drink and took a seat across the desk from the President. He took a sip from his drink, taking pleasure in the warmth that was spreading through him. "What's up, Mike?" he asked his oldest friend.

"Atlantis has maybe a year to survive. We need to explore the surface Jim. Otherwise, all life down here will end. The geo-thermal vents are on the verge of a major collapse. So we have to explore the surface, find out if it can support life and get our people up there within the next year. According to Dr. Roddenberry in geo-science, we've got six months to a year before the vents collapse and Atlantis goes dark," Shaw explained.

"Wow, Mike. That's a lot to take in," Thatcher took a long pull at his drink.

"It is, Jim. I need you to pick members to be part of the Surface Expeditionary Force. They will be accompanying a band of scientists who will determine if the surface world will be viable for colonization," Shaw replied.

"Damn," Jim Thatcher replied.

Mike Shaw took a long pull at his drink. "Yep, to say the least."

"Mike do you know what you are asking?" Thatcher looked at him.

"I do, Jim. More than you know."

Dr. Andrew Roddenberry looked at the fifteen scientists that had assembled in the room. He was very pleased to see that both of the Seavers had shown up. "Hello, colleagues. I know most of you are curious about why I have called you here.

"Most of it has to do with a dire threat to Atlantis Base. We are facing a crisis on at least two fronts. One is the very population of Atlantis itself. The other is the fact that the geo-thermal vents are crumbling, about to collapse. When that happens, Atlantis will lose all power."

"If Atlantis goes dark, the air will stagnate and the temperatures at this depth will cool the cities rapidly and anyone still inside will die. As most of you know, Life in the domes will end within hours, not days. At that point we will have no choice but to move to the surface," Roddenberry explained.

"Are you telling us that Atlantis is doomed, that there is no choice but to go to the surface?" Dr. Thomas Seaver asked, standing. Maria noticed that the buzz of questions and conversation stopped when her husband spoke.

"That is precisely what I am telling, Dr. Seaver. I have been tasked by President Shaw with putting together a team to accompany the Surface

Expeditionary Force to see if the surface is indeed habitable and ready for colonization," Roddenberry replied.

"How much cooperation can we expect from the Navy given the urgency of this mission?" Professor Benjamin Morales asked. He looked angry at what had been revealed.

"President Shaw has promised me full co-operation. You are all experts in your fields. However, you will have to complete a two week survival course under Naval supervision. Those of you who accept this mission, will leave in a week for the surface base that has recently been established in the Bahamas Island chain," Roddenberry told them.

"That's not much time to prepare, Dr. Roddenberry," Thomas Seaver noted.

"You are right, it is not. However time is of the essence, Dr. Seaver. I will meet with each of you individually before you leave tonight. If you choose not to go, I understand and a replacement will be found. I will meet with each of you in alphabetical order. I expect your answer then," Roddenberry nodded and walked away from the podium.

Thomas Seaver turned to his wife, who looked pale and shocked by it all. "Maria," he whispered.

"Tom, what does this mean?" Maria looked up at him.

"It means we have no choice. We have to go to the surface world and see if it is possible to live there," Seaver told her, holding her close.

"You plan on going along, knowing you could die?" Maria looked up at him.

"How can I not go? You know I have always dreamed of seeing the surface world," Seaver whispered.

"I know," Maria fell against him, knowing in her heart that she would accompany her husband, but not because she wanted to go, but because he did.

"Who will be in charge of the expedition? From a scientific standpoint?" Dr. Benjamin Morales asked. Seaver shot him a look, knowing what was coming. Benjamin Morales was an anthropologist with delusions of grandeur. He was a man who coveted power. Such men were dangerous.

"I have several names in mind Benjamin. I'll be going over them and I will communicate the top names in the morning. Now, it's getting late and I know you all have a lot to think about and talk over. This meeting is adjourned," Roddenberry replied, leaving Ben Morales scowling.

"Let's go home," Thomas Seaver told his wife as he took her hand and pulled her to her feet. Maria smiled, her own mood lightened by the excitement in her husband's eyes.

"Yes," she smiled back, her own eyes full of promise. Together the Seavers' walked out of the meeting hand in hand.

"Was that what you expected when you were summoned to that meeting?" Maria asked a couple of hours later as they lay beneath the sheets of their bed.

"Not really, but I wasn't exactly surprised by it either. I've mentioned the temperature fluxes and rolling brown outs the various domes have been undergoing. That the vents are collapsing after five hundred years, not a great surprise given the amount of energy each of the domed city-states consumes on a day to day level. What surprises me is that it didn't happen sooner," Tom replied.

"Are you really that anxious to risk the surface world?" Maria rolled over to face her husband who lay supine on his back, his hands beneath his head.

"The way I see it, the greater risk is staying down here. Right now, we're caged by the domes. The environment outside is deadly and harsh, between predatory creatures to the crushing weight of the ocean's depths. On the surface we stand a chance. I've watched some of the video from the Navy's exploratory missions. It is a brand new world out there, Maria. One just waiting to be explored. It will mean a whole new kind of life for future generations," Thomas replied

"You make it sound so…enticing, Tom. But what about

the dangers? Mutated forms of wildlife, mutated possibly even poisonous or carnivorous plants?" Maria asked softly.

"Exploration of a new world is always full of dangers, Babe, but if we don't explore we can never know what is out there. And the alternative to die down here in the cold and dark as the air runs out."

"When you put it that way, I guess there really isn't much of a choice is there?"

"Not really, no," Tom Seaver replied.

Kevin Cullhane picked up the Fleetwood Mk 5 Sonic Pulse Assault Rifle. It was the latest evolution of military assault rifle developed by the Defense Armory Research Potential Agency. They had been using similar devices and technology for years, but not in a real world environment. As the primary weapon of choice for the Surface Expeditionary Force, all members of the team and the civilian scientists would need to be checked out on it as well as the Fleetwood MP 75 PSP, a hand held weapon that could fire up to 1,000 sonic pulses before requiring a change to a fresh energy pack.

As team leader for the expeditionary force, it was his job to check out each of the weapons as well as the military body armor that his people would be wearing. He was impressed with the real-time heads up display in the helmets. He hoped they would be as effective on the mainland as they were on the islands that had been pretty much scrubbed of life by the storms and tsunamis more than 500 years before.

He pulled the rifle to his shoulder, aiming through the heads' up display. He looked through the display in the helmet at the drone target that was charging out of the brush at him. His finger touched the firing stud and the drone exploded in a nearly blinding flash. Cullhane frowned. The flash had over-whelmed the visual display for about two seconds, more than long enough to get a sailor killed by a determined enemy attacking in force.

Cullhane called up another drone, shooting quicker this time and the flash from its destruction was less of a problem. He would talk to Dr. Franklin about it. He was the one that had configured the sensors in the heads up display. He would need to make the corrections in the programming. Cullhane removed the battle helmet and sighed.

He liked the feel of the sun on his skin, liked feeling its warmth far more than he liked living in the cold and unforgiving depths of the ocean. Given a choice, no matter what the danger, he would choose to live life on the surface.

10

Dr. Ben Morales was fuming at his dismissal by Dr. Roddenberry. Names were being considered. What bullshit! He deserved to lead the mission! Who better than an anthropologist to determine if it would be possible to live on the surface with whatever life remained? He threw the glass he had been holding and it shattered, the liquor that it still held splashing against the wall

He touched the comlink, calling the one man that could over-ride any of Roddenberry's objections or recommendation…

Dr. Andrew Roddenberry sat at the desk in his home office. He had left the Geo-Sciences department several hours before. He rubbed his eyes. It had been such a long day. Ben Morales was going to be a problem. He had a lot of friends in high places and a lot of political clout. He had no doubt that the arrogant anthropologist would get himself appointed head of the mission. The question was how to temper him? Who would be the best foil to Morales?

Roddenberry smiled. Dr. Thomas Seaver. A perfect choice! Seaver was a popular man among the science community, a biologist and historian who would counter Morales ambition with caution.

Yes, it would be perfect! Knowing there was little he could do to prevent Morales from being named as the civilian head of the expedition, he would make Seaver his second in command, knowing that most of the scientist on the surface expeditionary force would follow Seaver's lead!

Chief Jean McKinney shouldered the energy pack for one of the laser pulse rifles. Like her Captain, she was working with robotic drones for targets. McKinney was a tall slender redhead with shoulder length hair pulled back into a ponytail. Even under the battle armor one could tell her body had good muscular development. One of the drones rolled into view and she fired, the red pulses burning through the air, causing the target to explode. The flash momentarily over-whelming the head's up display in her battle suit. Jean fired again as she waited for the visual display to reboot, spraying the laser pulses around and hitting at least two more drones.

Chief McKinney frowned as she stopped letting the display finally catch up. She growled angrily as she tore off her helmet, her words making some of the other sailors working around her blush. She would be speaking directly to Dr. Franklin about the problem with flash and the visual sensors. "Something wrong, Chief?" Cullhane asked politely.

"The damn flashes from explosions are whiting out the internal screen and the head's up display. That could get us killed in battle if we have to fire blind," McKinney replied.

"I noticed the same thing. Put it in a report and get it to Franklin immediately. Until this glitch is fixed, the expedition is on hold," Cullhane replied.

"What will the Admiral say?" McKinney looked at him arching one eyebrow.

"He'll agree. Losing people isn't what this mission is about. It's about survival, and if we are handicapped by sub-standard equipment, survival is less a possibility. When you come back you can try one of these flechete guns. They solve the dense underbrush issue that the Fleetwood's have," Cullhane replied.

"I'll do that, Captain. When do we see the first batch of these civilians that we have to babysit?"

"We have a week to get ourselves up to speed before we start giving them their crash course. I've seen a partial list and there are two or three that should be pretty good, the rest will be P.I.T. A. trainees."

"P.I.T.A?" McKinney looked puzzled.

"Pain In The Ass," Cullhane grinned. McKinney rolled her eyes and headed for the lab where Dr. Franklin was fine-tuning the new battle-armor.

Doctor Simon Franklin looked up as the door to the research center banged open and the angry looking red-head in nearly full battle armor stormed into his domain. His blue eyes widened slightly and he felt a trace of anxiety as she seemed to charge at him. Nervously running his fingers through his shaggy black hair he asked, "May I help you?"

"The head's up display in these helmets are crap, Doc. Any sort of flash overwhelms the screen and leaves us blind for nearly half a minute before it kicks in again.

That's thirty seconds too long to be firing blind when the shit is hitting the fan," Jean McKinney growled.

Even when not in full battle armor Jean McKinney was a formidable and fierce-looking woman, but in the armor it was amplified and Franklin was certainly not used to being accosted by a battle ready Amazon in his own lab. He stood there for a long moment, mouth hanging wide, as he tried to think of a response.

Finally he closed his mouth, took a deep breath and let it out slowly, very aware of the impatient attitude of the beautiful you woman in front of him. He extended his hand for the helmet. "May I?"

"You may," McKinney handed it to him. Franklin carried it over to a nearby work table and sat it down.

"Give me a moment to adjust the settings here. It should really be a very simple matter to fix it," Franklin said without looking at her as he worked both hands inside the helmet. McKinney couldn't help but grin, though she hid it quickly when he glanced fearfully in her direction. The doc was kinda cute in a nerdy sort of way.

"There, that should do it," Franklin said, turning and handing her the helmet back.

"I'm going to go try it and see Doc. Why don't you come out and see how these things actually perform in the field?"

"I'd like that, actually," Franklin told her.

"Then come along," McKinney nodded her head and then started for the door. She slipped the helmet over her head, giving it a moment for it to seal to the gel-lined bodysuit worn beneath the armor. Franklin followed her out the door.

A13

Thomas Seaver turned off the computer in his office. He had been reading the daily news reports and was appalled by what he had seen. News had leaked and there were protests springing up in each of the domed cities calling for the impeachment of President Shaw for even suggesting the expedition to the surface. A couple of small riots had even broken out over in Atlantis Three.

The unrest had been growing within the domed cities since the expedition had been announced, it seemed like someone was deliberately spreading unrest among the domes. He had a couple of ideas about that, they had formed once Roddenberry had released his list of scientists for the expedition and Ben Morales had found out that Seaver was going to be his second in command on the expedition. Morales had been less than pleased with the news and even less pleased to find out that the Navy were the ones really in charge.

Seaver grinned at that particular memory. He had been there when Morales had gotten the news. Still, it had prompted him to start carrying his Great, great, great, great, grandfather's Browning 9mm when he left the apartment that he and Maria shared. He had tried to convince her to carry one of the antique guns as well, but she had refused. Her comment being, "I'm a scientist, Thomas, not a gun-slinger or a spy."

"Neither am I," he had told her. "I'm just a man who likes to be prepared for what can happen." Maria had given him the cold shoulder the rest of the night. One day, she would learn to trust him. It was sad that after five years of marriage that hadn't happened yet. He slipped some papers into his briefcase and took the Browning from his desk drawer and stuffed it into the waistband of his pants. His jacket covered the gun as he stepped out of his office and locked it.

The building seemed unusually quiet tonight. Seaver glanced around, noting that the floor was empty. The short hairs on the back of his neck began to rise; an almost instinctual reaction to danger. The antique pistol was in his fist, his thumb wiping down the safety as the elevator opened and three armed men stumbled out. Seaver's gun was up, his finger squeezing the trigger instinctively. Flame and lead exploded from the Browning and the first of the men tumbled backwards as the other two swung to face him.

Thomas Seaver wasn't standing still, however. Moving forward, he fired again and again, dropping the other two. Seaver kicked their weapons away and searched them. He was not surprised by the fact that they carried no identification. It was an assassination team. The question was; who had sent it? He reached for him comm badge.

14

"Tell me again why you were armed, Dr. Seaver?" Civilian Security Force Sergeant Alix Davidoff asked.

"I've been following the news reports and I am also one of the co-commanders for the scientific personnel going on the surface expedition. I felt it prudent to protect myself," Seaver replied.

"You were expecting an attempt on your life?" Davidoff raised an eyebrow.

"Not expecting no, but I believe in being prepared for what can happen," Seaver shrugged.

"None of these so-called assassins managed to get off so much as a shot. Yet you claim you fired in defense of your life. How can that be?"

"Let me ask you a question Sergeant. If three armed men came off an elevator carrying weapons and you were the only one around and had the means to protect yourself, what would you have done?" Seaver glared at him.

"Tom, Tom Seaver! Are you okay?" a man wearing a Navy uniform stepped into the police interrogation room.

"Get out!" Davidoff glared at the man.

"Kiss my ass, Sergeant! I'm Admiral James Thatcher and this

man is under my command. You will release him at once!" Thatcher ordered.

"This is a civilian matter," Davidoff started, but Thatcher cut him off.

"No it is not, Sergeant. Under the national security act I am ordering you to release this man at once. If you disobey me, you will find yourself under arrest and subject to the Military Code of Universal Justice," Thatcher glared.

"Fine," Davidoff grumbled, knowing he was beat. He looked at Seaver. "You are free to go, but your weapon is evidence. It will remain here."

"The Hell it will," Seaver came up off his chair.

"Give the man his gun, Sergeant, or my men will break down that door and throw you in irons," Thatcher glared once more. Fire blazed in the cop's eyes but he handed over the weapon. Seaver stuffed it into his waistband, grabbed up his briefcase and followed Thatcher out of the room.

"Thank you Sir," he told Thatcher.

"Thank Dr. Roddenberry. He tipped me off as to what was going on. He thinks Ben Morales was behind this attempt on your life," Thatcher confided.

"It wouldn't surprise me," Seaver shrugged. "Ben and I have never exactly seen eye to eye on most things."

"Sounds like he might make a bad enemy," Thatcher observed.

"Then again, so might I," Seaver shrugged again. "I don't much give a damn."

"I can see that, Dr. Seaver. Be on your guard. This likely will not be the last attempt before the expedition launches. Be careful, Dr. Seaver. Be very careful. You leave for survival training in less than a week," Admiral Thatcher nodded.

"Aye, Sir," Seaver acknowledged, nodding his head. Together the two men waked out of the police station. Alix Davidoff watched them go, trembling with rage. How dare that over-blown Sailor threaten him and take his prisoner! He stormed back to his desk and picked up his private comm line and punched a number from memory.

"Your men failed. Seaver is alive and unharmed. Your men are all dead. I think he might be more formidable than you originally thought," Davidoff said coldly.

"Don't worry Sergeant. Once that mission leaves for the surface, we will take over the domes. My people on the Leviathan will make sure it never returns to Atlantis, nor will any member of the expedition! They want the surface, it is where they will die!" replied the voice at the other end.

"What are my orders?" Davidoff asked, still smarting from his confrontation with Admiral Thatcher.

"Keep an eye on Seaver and any other members of the surface party. Help sow dissent where you can. I understand that Professor Morales and Dr. Seaver do not get along well. See what you can do to worsen their relationship," ordered the voice at the other end.

"Aye, Sir. Your will be done," Davidoff replied, breaking the connection. If that was what the Supreme Leader wanted, that was what he would do. Davidoff hit his intercom. "Send in Stasher and Loeb. I have a job for them." Then he sat back in his chair to wait.

15

"Thomas, are you all right?"
Maria Seaver ran to her husband as
he entered their apartment, pausing
to lock the door securely behind
him. He turned and swept her into
his arms, kissing her hard as he
pulled her to him.

"I'm alive Maria, which is more
than I can say for the men who tried
to kill me," Thomas told her.

"Tried to kill you? My God,
Thomas! Tell me what happened!"
Maria tugged him towards the living
room. Thomas Seaver stripped off

his jacket and tossed it onto the coat rack. His pistol was still stuffed into his waistband as he dropped into his favorite chair, a battered old recliner that had once been his father's. Maria walked back carrying two bottles of his favorite beer, a microbrew that had moved beneath the waves five hundred years before called Killian's Red. Thomas Seaver twisted off the lid and took a long pull.

"I was leaving my office and noticed that the floor was empty. Then three men came out of the elevator with guns aimed at me. I drew my weapon and fired, got them all before they managed to get a shot off,' he told her.

"Thomas! You could have been killed!" Maria's hand went to her mouth.

"Now do you understand why I want you to carry a gun as well?" People are divided about this trip to the surface. Some are convinced it's a hoax, they don't believe that the geo-thermal conduits are fragmenting and collapsing. They think it is an excuse to force them to the surface to die. We know the truth, but they don't want to believe it," Seaver explained to his wife.

"I understand but I don't like it. Do you truly believe we are in danger?" Maria asked.

"What more proof do you need, Maria?" Tom looked at her as he drained his bottle of beer.

"I—God Thomas are you sure it is worth it?" Maria looked stricken.

"It will be the end of us if we don't Maria. All life in the domes will end and it will end horribly," Seaver said, standing. He walked to the kitchen and got another beer, then walked back to his chair. Twisting off the top of the bottle he dropped back into his seat.

"I'll consider carrying the gun, Thomas," Maria said at last.

"Thank you," Thomas Seaver said, but it wasn't only to his wife. Part of it was to God for getting through to her.

Captain Kevin Cullhane lifted the Sonic Pulse Assault Rifle and fired at three different drones, each of which exploded but without the white out flash of the day before! He grinned inside the helmet and slipped back under the waves. The re-breather gills in the suit kicked in immediately pulling oxygen from the sea-water, totally eliminating the need for bulky oxygen tanks. Two more drones charged under the water and he fired again, blasting them both to pieces.

As expected, the sonic weapons worked even better under the water because water itself amplified the already amplified sonic pulses. He let the rifle fall on its sling and snatched the MP 75 Personal Service Pistol from the magnetic sheath on his thigh and fired four rapid pulses, shattering a coral outcropping. Cullhane grinned again. Franklin had worked the bugs out all right!

Of course, Chief McKinney had a lot to do with that, he thought. It had surprised him at first; that the Chief would be attracted to the nerdy looking professor, but techs were techs and McKinney was a tech to the bone! He smiled, glad to know his Chief was human after all.

There had been times when he had wondered.

Admiral James Thatcher stepped aboard the ship that would be his home for the next several months. The U.S.S. Leviathan was huge, allowing not only for a more than 500 person crew and even families, it could also serve as an aircraft carrier for planes that it carried in its bowels. It carried missile batteries as well as nuclear-tipped torpedoes and surface cannons. He took in a deep breath and let it out slow. The big sub was at least as wide as two of the old surface aircraft carriers with her almost catamaran design and the turbine tube that ran though the middle of the undersea vessel.

"She's a beauty, Admiral," Captain Tom Burris declared, causing the Admiral to jump. He turned to face the captain.

"Not nice, Tom," Thatcher grinned.

"Perhaps not, but this baby is ready for a shakedown cruise. She's the largest undersea submersible vessel ever built," Burris said.

Admiral James Thatcher followed Captain Tom Burris as the younger man began the guided tour of the submarine that would likely be their home for the next several months if not years. The Leviathan was the largest undersea/surface capable vehicle ever built, able to house just over 1,000 crewmen and women and 500 scientists from various disciplines. It was a self-contained environment and nearly the equivalent of a mobile dome city, with both offensive and defensive capabilities.

Aside from serving as an undersea platform for further deep sea exploration, it could serve as a platform for surface exploration as well of the strange new world that awaited them. From scouting expeditions that had been sent out to remap what remained of the east coast, Florida was only a chain of islands. New York City was gone, many of the low lying states had lost part of their land mass to the sea. But Thatcher pushed those thoughts away, concentrating instead on the gleaming new Bridge. It was the heart and soul of the new submarine and even Thatcher had to admit it was a little daunting.

"My God, Tom. This is unbelievable! Holographic displays, camera fed real time imaging for a full 360 degree look, echotron sonar. It has everything I hoped for," Thatcher shook his head.

"It is amazing Sir," Burris agreed.

"How long before we take her out?" Thatcher asked, rubbing his hands in anticipation.

"We'll give her a brief shakedown transporting the scientists to Bermuda for their survival training, but the real tests won't begin until the mission does," Burris shrugged.

"While on that shakedown to Bermuda, I want every system and back up tested Tom. We will have a lot of folks depending on us and we cannot afford to fail. That means the new air squadrons and the deck launching systems and landing systems as well," Thatcher said.

"Aye, aye, Admiral, so noted," Burris grinned.

"Tom, this is going to be a magnificent adventure," Thatcher said, not realizing how prophetic his words were going to be.

19

"How dare you, Seaver!" Ben Morales stormed into his office his arms waving angrily in the air as Thomas Seaver looked up to see his secretary looking frightened in the doorway behind the man.

"How dare I what, Ben?" Seaver stood, coolly unfolding his six foot three frame from his chair and looming slightly over the shorter man.

"Telling the police I want to have you killed, just so you can take over the expedition!" Morales screamed, his face red and spittle flying from his lips.

"I suggest you calm down, Ben, and we discuss this like rational people. Because at the moment I have not idea in hell what you're talking about but I am sure as hell about to take offense to you busting into my office in such an undignified manner," Seaver said softly as he moved around his desk to confront the man.

Morales must have seen something in his eyes that he didn't like, because he suddenly took a couple of steps backwards and started gulping down air to get himself under control. "You sent the CSF after me saying I was behind the attack on you last night!" Morales gasped.

"Ben I did nothing of the kind. They were out to hang me for defending myself until Admiral Thatcher showed up to get me out of there. Was the guy you talked to named Davidoff?" Seaver asked, his voice still pitched low.

"He was one, there were two others. Stasher and Loeb. They roughed me up some, told me you had said I wanted you dead because you wanted to be in charge of the expedition," Morales growled.

"Ben, I could care less who's in charge. The mission itself is what's important. The domes will die if we cannot colonize the surface," Seaver told him.

"Then you aren't trying to cut me out of the expedition?" Morales looked puzzled.

"No, Ben. I think you need to report this incident to Admiral

Thatcher and see what he has to say," Seaver replied softly.

"Sure, I'll do that," Morales spun on his heel and walked out.

"I am so sorry, Dr. Seaver," Katie Smith, his secretary sobbed after the outer door to the office had closed. Seaver patted her on the shoulder.

"Don't worry about it Kid. Ben Morales is a world class jackass."

"Dr. Seaver!" she gasped in shock.

"Do you disagree with my assessment?" Seaver looked at her, grinning.

"Not at all, Dr. Seaver," Katie smiled back. Seaver turned and went back into his office and closed the door. He was just as glad that Morales had not gotten a look at his computer. Seaver had been studying the files of all the scientists picked to go on the expedition.

20

Ben Morales was smiling as he walked down the corridor to his own office. He didn't believe for a moment that Seaver had no ambition to take over the expedition once it reached the surface. Seaver was just too popular. He would have to make his own plans and see what he could do to discredit the biologist before the expedition even got underway! If not before they went for their survival training, then while they were undergoing it! Seaver had already proven himself to be a killer.

Morales wondered how many of the others would be uncomfortable about that?

Davidoff had given him a lot of ammunition there, unwittingly so but had given it to him nonetheless! According to the Sergeant of the Civilian Security Force, Seaver had murdered three men in cold blood the night before, and Seaver had not denied it. He could use that against him. Morales smiled. He had people to contact and campaigning to do…

Kevin Cullhane was just emerging from the water after a training exercise when the sensors in his helmet picked up the sound. He had never heard it before, but knew it was not natural. He looked up, searching the sky. Then he saw it. Twin condensation trails high in the sky above. An aircraft of some kind, obviously not one belonging to the Atlantis fleet. He walked backwards until only his faceplate was above the water.

It could mean only one thing. Others had survived the cataclysm 500 years before. The question was would they be friends or enemies? He also wondered if they had spotted the surface base on the island? There was no way to know about that. He once more made his way towards shore.

Cullhane knew he had to notify Atlantis Base about the plane. It was information that they didn't have, but that they needed. It meant that there were others out there on the surface!

President Shaw looked up as Albert Putnam walked into his office. Putnam was sweating and that in and of itself was unusual. "Albert, what is it?" Shaw asked.

"We have communication from the surface base," Putnam said, seeming almost to quiver while standing still.

"Well?" Shaw looked at him.

"Well what, Sir" Putnam returned the President's look.

"The communication, Putnam?" Shaw looked exasperated.

"Oh yes. One of the Marine Surface Expeditionary Force members stationed on the surface base spotted an aircraft on a high recon profile," Putnam stammered.

"So there is life up there," Shaw mused.

"It appears so, Mr. President," Putnam replied.

"Then the question is, Albert, how do we make contact with them?"

"It is, Sir."

"Get Admiral Thatcher on the line for me would you," Shaw commanded.

"Yes, Mr. President," Putnam replied, spinning on his heal and exiting the Oval Office. Shaw didn't notice the frown on Putnam's face as he left the room. A moment later his phone rang. Shaw picked it up. "Admiral Thatcher on the line," Albert Putnam's voice announced.

"Jim, I just got your report," Shaw was saying as Putnam hung up his receiver and headed to his own office. Once there, he dialed a special number that would forward his call through three different relays.

"Report," said the cold voice on the other end of the line.

"I just got word that there is another civilization on the surface. This could create problems for us," Putnam said, his fist white on the receiver.

"Perhaps, perhaps not. If this other group is unfriendly, they might actually further our cause. Keep me updated on new developments. I will pass this along to the Supreme Leader," the cold voice replied.

"For the Supreme Leader," Putnam said, breaking the connection.

Roddenberry was sitting at his desk when Tom Seaver walked in. "Got a minute?" Seaver asked.

"For you Tom, certainly. How are you doing? I heard about the incident the other night," Roddenberry replied.

"Thanks for sending Thatcher to rescue me. The CSF Sergeant was determined to hang me if he had the chance," Seaver replied.

"It was the least I could do seeing as how I got you into this mess," Roddenberry waved him off.

"Did you tell the CSF about Morales?" Seaver asked.

"Certainly not! When they notified me, I called Jim Thatcher," Roddenberry replied, looking upset.

"Then why did Sgt. Davidoff mention him during my interrogation?" Seaver mused.

"Good question, Thomas," Roddenberry agreed, suddenly understanding.

"Ben came to my office today and accused me of sicking Davidoff on him. Yet I never mentioned Ben Morales to him," Seaver explained.

"You think someone is trying to sabotage the mission to the surface?"

"I do. Have you noticed the reports about the growing unrests in the undersea cities about this expedition? Someone wants to stop it before it ever happens," Seaver said.

"So it seems, Thomas. Do you have any theories?" Roddenberry asked.

"I'm afraid I don't, Dr. Roddenberry. But I think someone should let President Shaw know that there is someone who doesn't want the expedition to happen," Seaver replied.

"That sounds very reasonable, Thomas," Roddenberry nodded.

"I know Ben Morales is campaigning to get me removed from the expedition. I think it would be a big mistake if he succeeds," Seaver said at last.

"So do I Thomas, so do I," Roddenberry replied.

President Shaw stood looking out the window of his undersea White House. His hands were clasped behind his back. It was a lonely time. Not even one he could share with his beloved Pamela or his children. There was other life on the surface. Another society as advanced as theirs.

But were they friendly? Or were their ideologies radically different? The only way to know was to make contact, and that couldn't be done until the Surface Expeditionary Force had left on their mission. He sighed.

Life on the surface, what would it mean? Colonies to say the least, before a gradual move to the surface. But how will people adapt? He knew that there were some who were violently opposed to the expedition, and they were stirring up unrest in all of the domed cities.

Both Civilian Security Forces and Military Units were moving to suppress the unrest, but there was no way to guarantee that they would be successful. He shook his head as he took a drink of the fine Bourbon he had poured for himself. President Shaw sighed softly.

A26

The man who called himself the Supreme Leader sat in shadows, the room sealed and quiet. His blue eyes glittered in the small amount of light that penetrated the darkness. His skin was pale, as was his hair. He contemplated the shadows as he thought about the latest intelligence that he had been given. Life on the surface, and apparently an advanced society enough to have advanced aircraft. It was a surprise.

Something he had hadn't prepared for.

He did not like being caught unprepared. Too long had he and his people been oppressed by the yoke of a so-called free and democratic society. But the time had arrived for them to step up and take over, to rule the undersea cities with an iron fist! Already his people were out in all the domes, stirring up unrest and anger about the surface expedition. However it was not enough!

He had decided to let the Leviathan leave Atlantis One. He had people on board ready to act as saboteurs to make sure that neither the sub nor the expedition ever returned. Perhaps it might be better to wait until they had made contact on the surface, see what the others were like and if they followed an ideology similar to his own. If so, they could be valuable allies against President Shaw and his Naval forces! He had much to think about...

A27

Maria Seaver ducked as a bottle shattered against the public transport that she was riding in. Outside she could see protesters waving signs and throwing more bottles. Glass ones shattered against the transport, plastic ones bounced harmlessly away. More and more she was beginning to understand her husband's interest in both survivalism and reaching the surface. The domes were starting to become very dangerous places!

She thought about the small .22 caliber pistol in her purse and she slipped her hand inside to wrap her fingers around the pistol's grip. She was surprised at the degree of comfort she drew from such a simple act. Perhaps Tom was right. Where before she had felt the domes were a peaceful haven, she now saw them as stifling and threatening as more riots seemed to break out daily. Not surprisingly, more and more protests were surrounding the science centers.

As the transport raced away from the Botany labs where she worked, it left the protestors far behind. Maria sighed with relief. She was glad to leave the violence behind her. There was, however, one very important thing she had to do after she got home. She would

tell Tom that she was sorry for
doubting him.

28

"Chief, I want two man patrols out, both surface and sub surface tonight," Cullhane told Jean McKinney.

"Any particular reason?" McKinney arched an eyebrow. It was a gesture that he sometimes loved, sometimes hated.

"I've got a bad feeling. That aircraft I saw today? I think I was meant to see it, which means somebody knows we're here.

Somebody besides Atlantis One," Cullhane replied.

"You think we've been seen, then?" McKinney asked.

"I do. At the very least I am going to prepare as if we have. First rule of war, Chief. Plan ahead," Cullhane told her.

"Good rule, Boss," McKinney nodded, heading out to give the orders. She trusted Cullhane's instincts. She had worked side by side with him long enough as a member of his team that she could almost anticipate his actions and orders before he gave them. If he thought there was going to be trouble, she was willing to bet that there would be trouble. She was beginning to wonder if their team might have its very first real firefight very soon!

Kevin Cullhane stripped off his camouflage Battle Dress Utility fatigues and climbed into his black smart-gel body suit. Once inside it, he began strapping the sea-blue ceramic battle armor in place. Sleeping comfortable tonight was out of the question, but sleeping ready? Oh yeah, that was the order of the day!

He checked his SPAR as well as his PSP and both were fully charged and ready. He had spare energy magazines at the ready for both weapons. If he was right, he would need them before the night was out. His Marines would get a trial by fire before the dawn. He was sure of that. He grabbed his helmet and headed out the door.

Kevin Cullhane slipped on his helmet, hearing it seal to the smart-gel body suit. He could hear

McKinney barking orders as he slipped through the shadows and walked out into the depths. As the water closed over his helmet, the mechanical gills kicked in, allowing the suit to draw oxygen from the sea water. Cullhane found a depression in the coral and settled in to wait…

Chief Jean McKinney cracked orders like a whip and was rewarded with the sight of assholes and elbows. The sailors scrambled to get into battle gear and get set in formations, so they could prepare for the expected "sneak attack," from the unknown people that apparently survived the holocaust that had wiped civilization from the face of the earth.

She was already armored up and ready. Patrols were something she would figure out as the time came. She had already sent four men out on Seahorse Scout vehicles to scan the harbor of the island.

McKinney didn't really expect the assault to come from the sea, however. She expected it to come from the air, paratroopers most likely. She had tasked three elements to keep an eye on the sky, and four guards to watch the ocean approaches to the island.

More than likely, any attack that came would come from the sky, paratroopers dropping in from above, using black parachutes to help them blend with the night and landing in areas away from the buildings. It made sense. She would send her patrols outside the perimeter and still have some inside.

That way they could catch the attacking force in a cross-fire and chop them to bits.

Jean McKinney smiled as she began to put her plan together. She already knew that Cullhane would be leading the undersea element and what sort of dirty tricks he had in mind.

Kevin Cullhane kept in close touch with the undersea scout element. They were circling about a mile out. So far there was nothing to report. Calm seas made the watch an easy one so far. It also added to what he had figured about the attack coming from the air.

Chief Jean McKinney heard the sound of the first plane flying overhead. "Get ready and keep an eye on the sky," she called out to her troops over the secure commlink. "Roger that, Chief," each of the men replied.

McKinney saw the first dark blot in the sky and smiled within her mask. As she expected the attack was coming from the sky. She charged her SPAR and got ready for action...

"Boss, we got underwater movement," came the call over his headset.

"What kind of movement?" Cullhane asked, charging his SPAR.

"UDV from the sound," came the reply.

"Keep the Seahorses ready for attack. We can stop the Undersea Delivery Vehicles if we need to," Cullhane replied. Cullhane was a little surprised that the attackers were still using the old sea-sled style of underwater propulsion to pull them through the water. The seahorse undersea scout vehicles were not only more efficient, they could be computer guided leaving the rider free to use their SPARs or the onboard weaponry of the Seahorses.

"Twenty meters and closing, Captain," came in a report.

"Take them out," Cullhane ordered and his people went to work. Sonic pulses fired out at remarkable speeds, taking down the undersea attackers and their equipment. The explosions weren't loud but they were still audible and the shockwaves could be felt.

"We got 'em boss," came another call over the wireless comm unit built into the helmet.

"All of them?" Cullhane asked.

"What we didn't get the sharks and barracudas are finishing, and Boss, it ain't pretty to watch."

"Death never is," Cullhane replied soberly. "McKinney, how are things going top-side?"

"Nice of you to ask," McKinney replied as she fired her Spar and dropped yet another of the paratroopers as soon as their boots hit the dirt. Fifteen to twenty paratroopers were still in the air. McKinney and her people took them out as the sound of the plane disappeared into the night.

"Stand down but keep alert," McKinney ordered. "Captain?" she switched to a private channel.

"Go Jean," Cullhane said as he emerged from the waves.

"What happened?" McKinney asked.

"Two-pronged assault, but it failed," Cullhane replied. "Gather the bodies, we need to take a close look at them.

Dr. Thomas Seaver took a round about way home. Since the incident at his office, he had tried to vary his routine. What few people knew about him was that he was a thriller reader and one of his favorite series was a long out of print series about a survivalist who survived world war three and travelled the country to find his lost family. That character, a fellow named Rourke had always planned ahead. It was a lesson that Seaver had learned the hard way.

The books were written by an author that Seaver had come to admire, an expert in weapons and survivalism that had many articles and books to his credit.

"Oh Tom," Maria had cried when he walked through the door. She threw her arms around him as he swept her into his arms.

"Baby what's wrong?" Thomas asked.

"It's getting horrible at the lab. The protesters and demonstrators were starting to get violent. They attacked the transport tonight," Maria whispered, holding him tight.

"Were you hurt?" he asked, pushing her back so he could look at her, searching for any sign of injury.

"No, but I think if they will let us we should move onto the Leviathan as soon as possible."

"I'll call Dr. Roddenberry and see if I can get him to get it okayed," Seaver told his wife.

"Thank you," Maria whispered. Seaver headed for his office, closing the door behind him. So had concerns of his own he wished to discuss with Dr. Roddenberry. He had done some digging around after their earlier discussion about his confrontation with Ben Morales.

Morales had been against the mission to the surface from the outset, and Seaver was pretty sure that the man wanted to sabotage it, especially if he could do so before it ever launched

The Leviathan cut through the
waves. She was six days out from

Atlantis One. Admiral Thatcher was on deck scanning the horizon with binoculars. They were nearing the island where the shore party would take their survival training. So far, he was running with just the conning tower of the colossal submarine visible on the surface. He had no wish to give away the true size or capability of the massive submarine.

"See anything interesting?" Dr. Thomas Seaver asked coming up beside him.

"Not really Dr. Seaver, just a whole lot of empty sea," Thatcher replied.

"That's good though isn't it?" Severin asked.

"Perhaps. Reports from the Surface Base say they were attacked a few days ago by an unknown surface force. Even after close examination of the bodies, there was no way to identify where they were from."

"Which means we may face more trouble up there than we thought," Seaver observed.

"Possibly. You're an intelligent man, Dr. Seaver, do you honestly think we are he only group to survive the cataclysm?" Thatcher asked.

"The odds are against it." Seaver nodded.

"Yes they are."

"I think we may find a very mixed group of people on the mainland from savage barbarians to advanced societies. Maybe some civilizations with old prejudices that we no longer share, but which they might aim at us," Seaver shrugged.

"We'll reach the training and staging base by sunset. How do you feel about that, Doctor?" Thatcher looked at him.

"I think that a brave new world awaits us on the surface, and I think that we need to plan for any and every possible scenario."

"That's the answer I was hoping for. You are aware that Dr. Morales wants to skip the training altogether and proceed with the mission?" Thatcher asked.

"Dr. Morales is an idiot, but he is in charge. However in decisions that affect the safety of the expedition I do have a strong voice," Seaver acknowledged.

"I hope it is one that the members well listen to."

"I do to," Seaver replied.

34

"Tom, are we making a mistake?" Marie Seaver asked later that afternoon. She was sitting in their cabin drinking a cup of coffee.

"No, Marie. Our future lies on the surface," Tom Seaver reassured his wife. "But there are a lot of short-sighted people back home that are afraid of change, afraid of losing the false sense of security from living in the domes for the past 500 years."

"I'm afraid too," Marie sipped at her coffee.

"We all are, Babe, but we have to face that fear and look to the future, start thinking about what we can do rather than what we can't do. We need to plan and prepare for what we might find so that we can adapt and overcome," Seaver explained.

"You know, with you at my side, I feel safe," Marie told him, smiling.

"Glad to hear it," Thomas told her, reaching out to take her hand. Together they walked to the berth.

Kevin Cullhane looked up as Jean walked into the room. He was sifting over the after-action reports from the attack and the few documents that they had found on the bodies, trying to glean so idea of what they were facing and who the attackers had been.

"Anything?" McKinney asked, dropping into the chair across the desk from him.

"Not a damn thing that makes sense," Cullhane slammed his fist down in frustration.

"They, whoever they are, have at the very least high flying reconnaissance plans if not operational satellites flying overhead. That's the only answer of how they knew about us having set up a forward base here.

"The question is who are they and are their intentions hostile?" Jean looked at him and Cullhane nodded his head. She was right.

"Well attacking us pretty much signifies hostile intent," Cullhane pointed out.

"Yeah, yeah it does," Jean admitted shaking her head.

"So did you come in here for a reason?"

"I did. The Leviathan will be arriving within the hour so we can start survival training with the landing party."

"Fucking wonderful," Cullhane groaned.

"Smile boss, and remember, you volunteered for this duty," Jean slipped out of her chair and walked out of the room hips in full sway leaving Cullhane staring appreciatively after her.

He sighed. Survival training. Cullhane shook his head, wondering if any of the scientists knew one end of a gun from the other. More than likely not. He had a feeling it was going to be a long damn week!

A36

"We've arrived, Admiral," Captain Tom Burris announced. Thatcher climbed out onto the conning tower.

"My God, no wonder they called these islands paradise," Thatcher breathed.

"Yeah, they certainly are," Burris acknowledged.

"Is Cullhane sending out a boat for the trainees?"

"He is, and he is not happy about it."

"Being happy is not in his orders, Captain. Make sure he is aware of that," Thatcher ordered, winking at the captain as the first of the scientist climbed out onto the deck.

"Yes, Sir!" Burris snapped a salute.

"Well done, Admiral," Thomas Seaver grinned.

"I thought you would appreciate the touch of theater, Dr. Seaver," Admiral Thatcher grinned.

"I do, though I doubt if Professor Morales will," Seaver replied.

"Dr. Morales can kiss my ass for all I care."

"That would certainly be a sight to see," Seaver chuckled.

"Yes, but it would be most unpleasant for me," Thatcher grinned.

37

Cullhane stood on the beach looking at the scientists. Most of them were a sorry looking lot, but a couple or three looked like they might be up to what they were facing. He would find out soon enough. He nodded to Jean and she slipped around behind the scientists. She had a projectile weapon. She lifted it and fired it into the air. One of the scientist spun into a defensive crouch and attacked, driving a side kick into her abdomen that put her on the ground as he moved in and twisted he weapon out of her grasp and turned it on her.

"I wouldn't move because I don't know if this is loaded with live rounds or blanks," Thomas Seaver said. The rest of the scientists were looking at him with something approaching horror.

"Very good, Doctor…?" Cullhane left the question unfinished.

"Seaver, Thomas Seaver."

"The gun is loaded with blanks, but I thank you for teaching my chief a lesson in humility. We didn't think any of you would know how to react," Cullhane grinned.

"Sorry, Ma'am," Seaver safed the weapon and extended a hand to the female soldier.

"Thanks," Jean said, then she kicked up with her feet and pulled at him. Seaver went with her pull, driving his elbow into her temple to stun her and then rolling to his feet and covering her once more with the weapon.

"Play nice now," he almost whispered.

"Doctor Seaver, step to the head of the class," Cullhane grinned. "Jones, Wilson, haul the Chief over to sickbay and get her checked out."

Two sailors picked up the Chief's inert form and half-carrier, half-dragged it off to one of the concrete block buildings.

"Okay, you folks just got a taste of what can and most likely will happen. Of all of you, Doc Seaver was the *only* one who was prepared for the unexpected. Of all of you, he is the one who stands the best chance to survive this mission. I am here to teach you how to survive this mission. You will do well to follow Dr. Seaver's lead through the training if you want to survive," Cullhane told them.

"This is barbarism," one of the scientists said, looking highly offended.

"Your name sir?" Cullhane asked.

"Ben Morales," the man relied.

"You sir are a Fucking idiot! You do what you have to in order to survive. Even if it means shooting and shooting to kill. The mainland is a savage place and we have enemies we know nothing about. If you want to survive to complete your mission, you have got to be prepared to fight when threatened," Cullhane replied.

"That is nonsense, we are on a peaceful mission of scientific discovery. We will simply reach out to any people we meet and let them see we mean them no harm," Morales shook his head.

"And if one of those people wants to rip your skin off and eat you alive, what will you do to convince him you mean him no harm?" Cullhane asked, a sardonic smile on his face.

"I—you are twisting my words!" Morales snapped.

"No, Dr. Morales I am calling it like I see it. If you are not prepared to fight, I guarantee that you will die up here. The face of the world has changed in 500 years. If you want to survive, you will learn to fight. If you don't want toe fight, you will die," Cullhane said matter of factly.

"I don't believe it is that bleak," Morales shook his head.

"Really Sir?" Cullhane asked, stepping closer, deliberately crowding into the scientist's space. "Some of those on the surface may be civilized in the loosest terms, but a great many have reverted to barbarism and cannibalism. Our recons have found evidence. But if you want to go naked into the wilderness, be my guest. Just don't expect help when one of the new natives is cutting your guts out and eating them as you watch and scream."

"How many of you think like Doctor Morales?" Cullhane looked at the group. All but about three of them stepped back. " How many agree with Dr. Seaver and the example he presented?" The remaining members of the group stepped to the side. "You might stand a chance of surviving," Cullhane told them.

"I should have known you were behind this, Seaver!" Morales screamed suddenly. He lunged towards the other scientist. Seaver took two steps forward and snapped his foot up and out, catching the older man in the chest and driving him back. Morales hit the ground hard, but came up fast, flinging double handfuls of sand at Seaver but the younger man was prepared and side stepped most of it, meeting the older man's charge, turning his shoulder into his body as he levered the outstretched arm up and over his shoulder, sending the older and heavier man flying through the air to land hard on the sand. In two steps he dropped down hard, landing both knees in the older man's gut, driving all the air out of his body.

Seaver stood and walked a few steps away. He looked down at Morales. "Never attempt that again, Ben. Next time I'll kill you," Seaver said.

Ben Morales lay on the ground looking up at him, his eyes filled with hate. Cullhane stepped in. "Go stow your gear and hit the Mess Hall. Training begins in two hours. He looked down at Morales. "No exceptions." Then he turned and walked away. Seaver joined his wife and they headed towards the cabins that had been set up for married couples, of which there were five.

38

Jean was sitting up in sickbay when Cullhane walked in. She smiled ruefully. "So what do you think?" Cullhane asked her.

"That one is good, a natural leader too. Folks will follow him," Jean replied.

"So how did it feel to underestimate one of the geeks?" he teased.

"Painful," Jean rubbed her temple. "He caught me totally off guard. That hasn't happened in a long time."

"In my humble opinion, Jean, Doc Seaver is a natural. Good instincts, superior reflexes. He took you down twice with minimum effort. Anybody that follows his example, they might have a chance of surviving." Cullhane said.

"I believe that is a fair assessment. What about the team leader?" Jean asked.

"I think he was selected as cannon fodder," Cullhane replied honestly.

39

Atlantis One Seabase.

The President looked up as the head of the Secret Service walked into the Oval Office. "What is it Clarence?" Clarence Savage looked uncomfortable.

"We have uncovered a movement Sir. One expressly aimed at stopping the exploration of the surface and the exodus back to land," Savage replied. Savage was a large man, well muscled and imposing at well over six feet in height. He might be head of the secret service, but he was still flustered in the presence of his Commander in Chief.

"What does this group call itself?" President Michael Shaw asked.

"They have no particular name but the man at the head of the group is known only as The Leader," Savage replied nervously.

"What have you been able to find out about him?" Shaw looked at the head of the agency responsible for his and his family's security.

"Too damn little," Savage replied.

"That is not comforting," Shaw sighed.

"No sir, it is not," Savage agreed.

"I don't care what it takes, Clarence, find out all you can. These people need to be put down hard and fast," Shaw said.

"Yes, Sir," Savage replied, turning on his heel and walking out. President Shaw sighed as he watched him go. Anarchists were the last thing that Atlantis needed in this crucial point in her storied history. As much as he hated the idea, he might have to declare martial law until the expedition had returned…

40

The Leviathan, somewhere off the Bermuda Coast.

Admiral James Thatcher stood in the conning tower. He had a bad feeling about this mission, one that he had not yet shared with his officers.

He had also been listening to traffic from the news broadcasts from Atlantis One. Troubling times indeed. There was danger on the surface, danger that he hoped that they were prepared for. But there was danger back in Atlantis as well, and that might be the worst of it all.

Thatcher was enjoying the feel of the sun's warmth on his face and skin. But he also wondered if they would be called back to help defend Atlantis One from the dangers that were apparently growing within the undersea city. As it was, he was sending out patrols of mini-fast attack subs to make sure that the ship wasn't endangered by the enemy that had attacked the training and staging area. That was another reason why Leviathan had not totally surfaced yet during this shakedown cruise.

"Admiral?" a familiar voice called from behind him.

"Yes, Tom?" he turned to face the ship's Captain.

"We may have a saboteur on board. During one of the routine security checks, Ensign Frost found a bomb planted next to the main drive," Tom Burris sighed.

"Get security on it right away Tom. Have them sweep the entire ship, and I want intensive checks done on every member of the crew. If we have dissidents aboard, we need to know sooner than later," Admiral Thatcher ordered. Thatcher shook his head. Danger from within indeed!

41

Tom Seaver was sweating as he completed the two mile run around the island, but still doing better than most of the others with the exception of his wife. Maria was also in top physical condition and the pair had often run marathons in the domes. Morales was in the rear of the pack, not being in the best of physical condition.

"Are you sure it was wise, confronting Ben like that?" Maria asked.

"Wise, probably not. Necessary, very," Thomas Seaver replied.

"Yes, he made a big mistake in attacking you," Maria nodded as they ran.

"Yeah, Ben over-played his hand. He seems to becoming more unstable daily," Seaver nodded.

"So what are you going to do, Tom?" Maria shot a glance at him.

"Whatever I have to," Seaver shrugged as he ran.

42

Kevin Cullhane watched the
group as they ran. Seaver and his
wife were out front which was really
no surprise. They were the most
physically fit of the scientists.
Stromberg and Lynda Kane were
next. They were close to Seaver and
his wife and had shown an almost
natural proficiency with the weapons
and physical training. Not
surprisingly Dr. Morales and his
cronies brought up the rear looking

like they were completely spent, though slimmer than when they arrived. The physical conditioning had done the group of scientists some good.

"What do you think, Captain?" Master Chief Jean McKinney asked from his elbow.

"I think they might have a fighting chance if they get into trouble," Cullhane said grudgingly.

"Better than they had when they got here. Any new intelligence on who our attackers were?" McKinney changed the subject.

"Not really, but our surface contacts have been pretty limited," Cullhane sighed.

"We need to sweep the surrounding islands. They had to come from somewhere, and *The Leviathan* would have spotted any other boomers in the area," McKinney said.

"Pick four people and I'll contact the Admiral, see how he wants to do this," Cullhane said.

"Only four?" McKinney arched an eyebrow at him.

"You're going with them, along with a contingent from the ship. Ought to be enough to deal with any stragglers," Cullhane grinned.

"Aye, Sir!" McKinney grinned and snapped a salute and turned and headed out the door. McKinney touched his communication device. "Admiral Thatcher," he said.

43

"Dr. Seaver, a moment please," Chief Jean McKinney called out. Thomas Seaver looked up, brushing back a stray strand of hair that had fallen across his forehead in a dark comma.

"No hard feelings, Chief," Seaver smiled.

"No, but some dandy bruises, Doctor. I'm putting together a small team to sweep the surrounding islands. You've impressed a lot of us and we want you to go along," McKinney told him.

"I'm honored," Thomas Seaver said.

"But?" she asked looking at him.

"Do you think I'm really ready?" Seaver asked honestly.

"We do. I want to see how you react in the field Dr. Seaver. Training is one thing, but this is the real thing. I want to know what you'll do under fire. That will help me evaluate the mission's chances for success," McKinney replied.

"Okay. When do you want me to draw my equipment from the quartermaster?" Seaver asked.

"How about now? The boats will pick us up in forty-five minutes.

I need you suited up and ready at the docks ASAP," McKinney replied.

"I'll be there," Seaver told her. McKinney smiled as she watched him go. She wasn't sure Cullhane would approve, but she had a feeling about Dr. Seaver based on his performance in training and his actions defending himself at Atlantis Base before the expedition left.

44

The Quartermaster had his gear ready and waiting when Seaver walked through the door. The man helped him quickly don the smart gel suit and the additional armor. He checked the SPAR and the PSP and the energy charges for both. Finally he handed Seaver his helmet. "You've fifteen minutes," the Quartermaster told him. Seaver nodded, grabbed his helmet and headed out the door.

Seaver felt the butterflies in his stomach. This wasn't like the incident at the school. This time, he would be walking directly into danger with his eyes open and ready. He had wondered how the Marines did it. It looked like he was about to find out.

45

McKinney and three other Marines stood ready and waiting at the dock. Seaver joined them. McKinney eyed him. "Nervous?" she asked.

"Wouldn't you be?" Seaver met her gaze.

"Yeah, I would. You're not alone in that though. The Marines from *Leviathan* are as green as you are. They have to learn the same things you do so they can survive the expedition. You're in good company, Doc. Your wife is getting there but she wasn't quite ready for this," McKinney told him.

"No, she isn't. She won't be real happy with me when she finds out," Seaver smiled.

"She'll be fine if you come back alive," McKinney said.

"So you say," Seaver grinned. He knew Maria better than that!

If anything, he would be lucky if his wife would even speak to him for a week after finding out that he had gone on a mission without her. Seaver knew that he was being tested by the Marines. Why he wasn't sure about.

McKinney waved him forward to the fast attack submersible and Seaver strapped himself in. He quickly familiarized himself with the harness and how to disconnect it under battle conditions. His SPAR was clamped into place next to his seat. His PSP was holstered on his right hip. Seaver was surprised when McKinney took the seat beside him.

"I'm trusting you to watch my back," McKinney told him.

"I'll do my best," Seaver told her honestly.

"I know you will Doc. My Boss wants us to get the job done. I'm trusting you to make sure that you do," McKinney told him.

"What is going on in the domes," Seaver asked.

"Why do you ask?" McKinney looked at him.

"Do you think I'm that naïve?"

"No, Doctor I don't. There is a lot of sentiment against the mission to the surface. Most of them don't know that the geo-thermal vent is failing."

"I thought as much," Seaver nodded. "Why the resistance?"

"They are being manipulated," McKinney said.

"By whom?"

"I wish I knew," McKinney said.

46

Atlantis Base 1, beneath the Atlantic Ocean.

The man calling himself the Leader looked at his reflection in the window of his office. Tall, lean and powerfully built, a thick shock of blond hair neatly trimmed and styled. His shirt was tucked neatly into his slacks and contrasted against the dark fabric. A thin scar crossed his left cheek. He had a strong jaw and a long thin nose.

The Leader looked down through the window and smiled slightly at the crowd of people in the streets below, gathered to demonstrate and protest the mission to the surface. He imagined that President Shaw was not happy about the growing unrest.

Shaw was an old adversary, going back to their college days. Even then Shaw had been a do-gooder, always talking about equality and fair-play. But the Leader had never liked him. They had competed against each other in college. Shaw had given him the scar that marred his perfect good looks. The Leader could have had it removed but had instead chosen to keep the scar as a reminder of his enemy.

A chime sounded and the man known to his followers as The Leader turned. "Come in," he said. The door slid open. Bob Willis entered the room.

"There is rioting going on in at least two domes," Willis said without preamble.

"Excellent. What has the official response been?" The Leader asked.

"Shaw has stopped short of declaring martial law but it is only a matter of time. Our instigators are stirring people up and holding rallies against the surface mission. Once Martial Law is declared, we can battle him more openly."

"We need to push this. Have one of our units bomb one of the rallies. Make it look like it was police or military that did it. That should force Shaw's hand and stir the rebellion," The Leader folded his hands behind his back as he paced back and forth across the office.

"Bomb our own people?" Willis looked shocked.

"Sacrifices for the movement. They will be martyrs to the cause," The Leader said dismissively. "I want a list of our most dedicated members. I will personally select the men for this mission."

"As you command," Willis thumped his left fist against his chest and extended his arm, palm facing outward in salute, and then spun on his heel and left the room.

Behind him The Leader smiled. "And so it begins," he whispered.

ATLANTIS RISING

2

SURFACE ACTION

A sweep of the surrounding islands brings the men and women from Atlantis face to face with Neo-Nazis and pirates.

Meanwhile in Atlantis base the unrest is growing and the Leader prepares to bring his forces into the open and President Shaw and the government find themselves fighting for their lives...